MOMMA'S MAGICAL PURSE

Paulette Bogan

BLOOMSBURY CHILDREN'S BOOKS

Type set in Malloy
The art was done in ink and watercolors.
Designed by Marikka Tamura

Published by Bloomsbury, New York and London
Distributed to the trade by Holtzbrinck Publishers
Library of Congress Cataloging-in-Publication Data
Bogan, Paulette.
Momma's magical purse / by Paulette Bogan.
p. cm.
Summary: David doubts that Momma's purse is magical until trouble
strikes at a rainy picnic.
ISBN 1-58234-842-1 (alk paper)
[1. Handbags--Fiction. 2. Mother and child--Fiction. 3. Magic--Fiction.
4. Cats--Fiction. 5. Dogs--Fiction.] I. Title.
PZ7.B6357835 Mo 2004
[E]-dc22
2003047192

First U.S. Edition
1 3 5 7 9 10 8 6 4 2

Bloomsbury USA Children's Books
175 Fifth Avenue
New York, New York 10010

All papers used by Bloomsbury Publishing are natural, recyclable products made from
wood grown in sustainable, well-managed forests. The manufacturing processes conform
to the environmental regulations of the country of origin.

Love and thanks to Sophia, for all her help
And for our cool cousins,
Cassandra, Austin and Mackenzie

Cousin David never believed anything.
"My momma has EVERYTHING in her purse," said Rachael.
"She does not," said David.

"Everything," said Rachael.
"And the purse is magic, too!"
"It is not!" said David.

"Children, are we going to argue, or are we going to the park?"
asked Momma. She patted her purse. "Now come along."
Momma always had her purse.

Rachael scratched her knee on a branch.

"OUCH!" she cried. "Momma, I hurt my knee."

"Would a kiss make it better?" asked Momma.

"And a bandage," said Rachael.

David rolled his eyes as Momma pulled out a bandage. "Everyone has bandages," said David. "That's not magic."

It was windy by the lake.
"Brrr," shivered Rachael.
"Momma, I'm cold."

Momma dug in her purse. "Here, honey, try this," she said.

"That was just luck," said David.

"Thank you, Momma," Rachael said.

"You're welcome," said Momma.

"Momma, did you bring anything to eat?" asked Rachael. "We're getting hungry."

"Oh dear, it is lunchtime," said Momma, and she opened her purse.

"No way," grumbled David.

Momma pulled out a perfect picnic lunch.

"Here we go!" Momma said.
Rachael said, "See, it IS magic."

"Momma, why do you have so many things in your purse?"
asked Rachael.

"Well," Momma said, thinking carefully. "You never know
what you might need," and she smiled a mysterious smile.

David was not smiling.

All of a sudden it started to rain.

"Oh, dear," said Momma.
Soon umbrellas, galoshes, and raincoats were flying from her purse.

David was dry, but he was not happy. There was something fishy about this purse. He was going to have a look for himself.

"Let's see who can collect the most raindrops!"
said Rachael. "Momma, do you have a bucket?"
"Hmmm. Just a minute, honey," said Momma.
"Let me look."

Momma frowned as she rummaged through her purse.
"This purse needs a good cleaning," she said, pulling
out one thing after another.
Rachael looked worried. David looked in the purse.

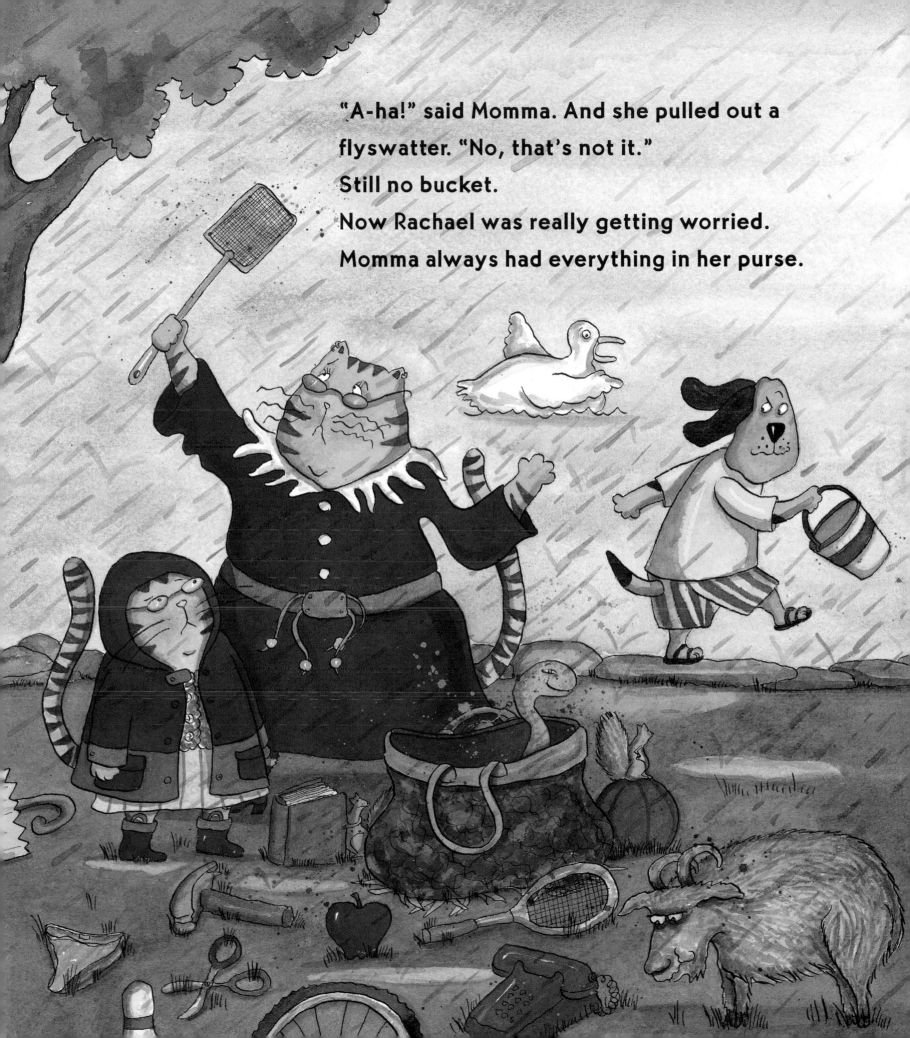

"A-ha!" said Momma. And she pulled out a flyswatter. "No, that's not it."

Still no bucket.

Now Rachael was really getting worried.

Momma always had everything in her purse.

"Where is David?" asked Rachael.
Suddenly they heard a whimper.

"That pup's in trouble!" said Momma.
"Watch my purse, Rachael, here I go!"
Momma pulled out her Rescue Kit.

Momma lassoed a log and stepped out onto the rope.

"Go, Momma, go!" Rachael called. "Be careful!"

"Aarrooo!" howled David.

"Don't worry, David. My momma's coming!" yelled Rachael.

Momma and David tiptoed back to shore.
"Yay, Momma!" said Rachael.

"This has been quite a day," said Momma.

"At least it stopped raining," said David.

"Momma," said Rachael. "I know what you need, and it's not in your purse."

Rachael gave Momma a big hug and a kiss. So did David!

"Thank you, sweeties," said Momma. "That's just what
I needed. Does anyone have a hankie?"

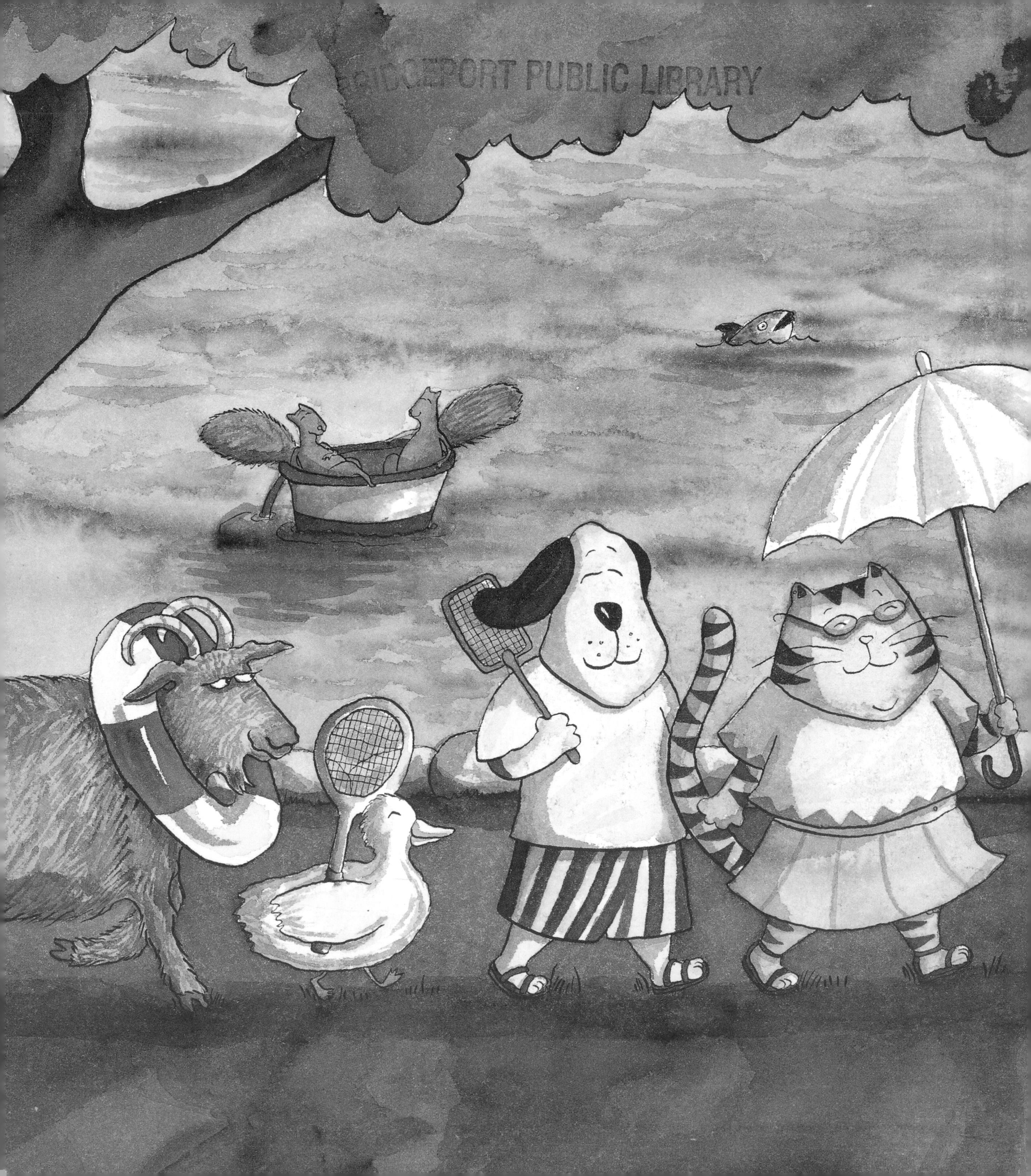